THE CRITICS ON C

Cecile Pineda is a writer of the utmost artistic integrity.
– J. M. Coetzee, Nobel Prize recipient

An author of powerful imagination and intellect, Cecile Pineda has already been compared to Cortazar, Borges, Marquez, Camus, Lagerquvist and Kafka. She has become one of the most discussed up-and-coming American novelists around.
– San Antonio Light

Critical Praise for *Bardo99:*

. . . Written in a style that crosses Kafka's paranoid paradoxes with the post-apocalyptic morality of Heironymus Bosch via William S. Burroughs, Bardo99 *is a fast-paced hallucinogenic trip [that] catalogues 20th-century human atrocities . . .*
– Education Digest

Critical Praise for *Face:*

A poetic, hallucinatory work, finely and sparely written, the debut of a very talented writer indeed. May we see more?
– Newsday

Written with sparse prose, stark drama and pointed symbolism, Face *is an intensely moving tale of catastrophe and redemption, of the fall and unyielding will of the human spirit. The prose of this novel cuts like a surgeon's scalpel; not a word is wasted or out of place.*
– Nashville Banner

There is an immediacy to her narrative, combined with images that startle our senses, that leave us haunted.
– San Francisco Chronicle

Critical praise for *Frieze:*

Elegant form and vigorous detail give Frieze *its mesmerizing power.*
– Josephine Humphreys in The Nation

As delicately phrased as a prose poem. . . . A parable that opposes the pride and power of the state to the slow resistance of human life.
– Richard Eder in The Los Angeles Times Book Review

Critical Praise for *The Love Queen of the Amazon:*

An outrageously inventive novel, the love child of Fanny Hill, fathered by some randy Latin American magical realist. . . . In a story that is shrewd, sensual, and beautifully crafted, [Pineda] serves up social satire surreptitiously disguised as a delicately off-color fable – a delight from cover to cover.

– Armanda Heller in *The Boston Globe*

The passionate backdrop of South America has produced some of modern literature's most remarkable female characters. . . . In her third novel, The Love Queen of the Amazon, *Cecile Pineda enhances this roster with a brilliantly drawn portrait of a Peruvian bawd, Ana Magdalena Figueroa. She is one of the few great Latin heroines not created by the male imagination, and Ana Magdalena's amorous history provides a unique vehicle for the U.S.-born Pineda to look with a satirically feminine eye at the manners, mores, and literature of all the Americas, to which* Love Queen *is a noteworthy addition.*

– Richard Martins in *The Chicago Tribune*

Ana Magdalena Arzate de Figueroa stars in Cecile Pineda's terrific new novel, The Love Queen of the Amazon. *Ana Magdalena's husband is writing a novel that goes by the same name, and her sailor lover's riverboat is called the Amazon Queen. . . . Her story has a soft, erotic feel, with a cast of characters who persist in making theatrical fools of themselves and others throughout. . . .*

– Tom Miller in *The New York Times Book Review*

On Cecile Pineda's new novel, *Fishlight: A Dream of Childhood:*

Fishlight *is a gentle, beautiful book, a rare and poetic song from an exquisitely melancholy childhood, written with heartbreaking innocence and a great love of life. It is original, poignant, profoundly simple and unforgettable. Cecile Pineda creates wonderful magic.*

– John Nichols, author of *The Milagro Beanfield War*

Fishlight *is a long-awaited treat. . . . full of pulsing, beautiful language from a gifted storyteller. . . . Cecile Pineda is writing at the peak of her craft. I revel in the open heartedness of this writer and I cherish her new novel.*

– Virgil Suarez, editor of *Iguana Dreams*

Redoubt

Other novels by Cecile Pineda

Bardo99

Face

Frieze

The Love Queen of the Amazon

Fishlight:
A Dream of Childhood

Redoubt

a mononovel

Cecile Pineda

San Antonio, Texas
2004

Redoubt © 2004
by Cecile Pineda

Cover illustration, "Cuerpo de Milagros, No. 5"
© 1997 by Kathy Vargas

First Edition

ISBN: 0-930324-86-2 (paperback)

Wings Press
627 E. Guenther
San Antonio, Texas 78210
Phone/fax: (210) 271-7805

On-line catalogue and ordering:
www.wingspress.com

Library of Congress Cataloging-in-Publication Data

Pineda, Cecile.
Redoubt : a mononovel / Cecile Pineda.-- 1st ed.
p. cm.
ISBN 0-930324-86-2 (trade pbk. : alk. paper)
I. Title.
PS3566.I5214R43 2004
813'.54--dc22

2004014923

Except for fair use in reviews and/or scholarly considerations, no portion of this book may be reproduced without the written permission of the author.

for Sydney Carson, colleague, cohort
and friend

Redoubt

Show me your face before you were born.
– Zen Koan

Faced with "the horrible dangers of war," Bernard Palissy contemplated a design for a fortress.... He journeyed through "forests, mountains, and valleys" to see if he could find "some industrious animal that had built some industrious houses." After inquiring everywhere, Palissy began to muse about "a young slug that was building its house and fortress with its own saliva." Indeed, he passed several months dreaming of a construction *from within*.

– Gaston Bachelard, from *The Poetics of Space*

I.

redouter (Fr.) (rədu-té) *v.t.*, To dread. To fear.

I **have been here** since the beginning. The road – if there were a road – leads nowhere. There are no ships in the desert. If there were oars or skiffs, they are gone, long since, along with the ghosts of the desert antelope. Their bones lie uninhabited everywhere. The harsh light of the sun has bleached them of any color. Nothing moves. There has been no rainfall in over one hundred years.

My position occupies the last line of defense on the frontier. I am charged with holding my ground, defending against the enemy. The redoubt stands, a dugout of reinforced concrete, its footings sunk in sand. The loophole hatches (there are two) can be raised or lowered at will by virtue of a mechanism of springs and counterweights. From within, I watch.

I know exactly where I stand. All around lies hostile territory. I have what weapons I need: compass, sextant, chart box. Detailed maps displaying latitude, longitude and topological formations. A gnomonic chart – of my own devising – showing my position as the polar center from which all points radiate. I take my readings, make entries in the logbook. Vigilance is the first order of defense on the frontier. The least shift of attention, a temporary lapse, merely momentary, may provide the fatal loophole, the opening in the skin, insignificant perhaps, unnoticed even, from which death may ultimately result. Strange things have happened. A paper cut merely, and the body fails. Communications falter. Infection spreads. There is irreversible collapse.

I live as best I can. By day, I keep to my routine: set the time, stow the sleepsack in the overhead loft. Crank open the hatch covers. Apply oil from time to time to keep the mechanism functioning and noiseless. Fumble – always manage to fumble – in one pocket or another for the key before positioning the leg iron. Fasten it securely. Prepare to take up my position from the night before. Raise the binoculars. Observe. Read my distance from the frontier, my proximity to the Capital. Or, in another manner of speaking, how close to the frontier, how distant from the Capital. I am alert to the slightest movement, armed against any occurrence, foreseen and unforeseen, charged with holding my ground, watching for the enemy. I have my instruments: compass, quadrant, sextant. I have my binoculars and I keep to my routine. It seldom varies, seldom. In the desert, nothing varies, even the sky, high, indifferent, cloudless without let-up. In this landscape there is nothing. Nothing and next to nothing. Endless days. Days without event. And yet. And yet. There is much to consider. Light. The shifting of light for example. Careful note must be made of light. Air currents. The movement of wind. Temperature. Relative humidity. Barometric pressure. Nebulosity: cirrus, cumulus, stratocumulus, or cirrostratus or cumulonimbus. Proportion of sky covered at dawn, at noon, at sunset. Day by day, month by month, year by year. Relation to temperature. Ombrothermic curves. Plotting their coordinates.

Empty routine? Hardly. Everything – in the relative scheme of things – everything has its purpose. Sand, for example. The movement of sand. Of critical importance. What is there if not sand? Not sea – or sky for that matter – yet it moves. Waves, waves rising and falling: crests and troughs – like breathing. Yes. A kind of breathing, mounding, yawning, prey to the ribbed patterns of maverick winds. Plowing surface under surface. Moving, never fixed.

The days here pass without respite. The dawn winds fan the night's chill air over the desert. By noon, the sun's heat sets the sands to gasping. The sky remains cloudless, harsh and uncompromising. Each hour of the day is like the hour of any other, always the same, or very nearly always. My routine never varies from sunup to sundown . . .

. . . never? without variation?

Perhaps there are momentary lapses, I admit, momentary lapses when the eyes falter, when the eyelids dream. Nothing deliberate. Not in any way deliberate. A momentary lapse. An insignificant falling off, say, of attention . . .

. . . a dream? A dream, perhaps?

Probably not. Probably nothing so deliberate. No warning beforehand. No warning when it is about to occur.

More a sensation.

A sensation at best. A falling. A kind of falling as if it . . . as if I . . . as if, in the relative scheme of things, hostilities, redoubt, nothing mattered. All, all had become no more than sand. Always there, yes, but never the same, never quite the same. Millions of grains, of particles, propelled by forces, some of them unknown as yet: wind, weight . . .

. . . and water?

And water, imagine. I could hear it lapping, lapping. Feel it rocking against the pilings. A momentary lapse. Perhaps not even a second. A fraction measured by the imperceptible drooping of an eyelid, recognized when, only a moment afterward, I opened my eyes. All was as before. Identical. The redoubt, the loophole hatches – still raised. It is not dreaming. I know only because afterward, when I open my eyes, I have no memory of dreaming, not in the strict sense. Not dreaming, not so much dreaming as a sensation, more a sensation as if I . . . as if a woman waited, crouched at the oarsman's bench, the oars shipped, idle in the oarlocks.

– Where are you going?

And she . . . no indication. A woman, a woman, certainly. Veiled. Dark. Dark clothing. Not quite black, or perhaps faded by the sun. No face. None discernible at any rate. Only the hands visible. Chalk-white – veins knotted like ropes – tightening over the oars.

– Not who she seems, not as she appears.

Who? Who then, I ask myself. Someone remembered? From another time, perhaps? Or someone unmet, as yet unnamed, hands veined thick as ropes. Bandaged. Against wound, perhaps? or gender – the dark welling?

– Where are you going? I asked, but could get no indication. Only the voice of the water, lapping, lapping against the pilings, the oars groaning in the oarlocks. A sign? I ask myself from where might it have come? Might it be a warning, a warning of things to come? Of what?

It has been calm in the desert of late. No visitors. None of any consequence. Of invasion, perhaps? But there have been no signs of hostilities, none of late at any rate – with the possible exception of the occasional volley of gunfire at sunset.

Strict vigilance is the rule on the frontier. I take my bearings. I keep to my routine.

Not always.

Not always then; not all the time. Sometimes I keep a tally of my dreaming . . .

. . . if you dare to call it dreaming . . . .

Not dreaming so much. Strange accounts of the body while it sleeps, the skiff that time riding at anchor, the wash of water against the pilings, the woman swathed in black – or some burned out color, faded by the sun. Or dreaming of night, for example. Waiting for the moment when the light exhausts itself, the last infinitesimal glimmer before the dark when the sky – what I can see of it – takes on its final color, not color in a strict manner of speaking, more a gloaming, the last reach of day before the night. A door closing, a temporary respite. Time to lower the loophole hatches (there are two), to light the lamp. To sit at the field commander's desk recording entries in the logbook. Latitude in the latitude column, longitude in the longitude column. Or amuse myself watching wild dogs snarl at the play of shadows my hands cast upon the walls. Start to the cry of some furred desert animal surprised by the talons of the owl.

At such times I wonder: can it be the war is over? Can hostilities have ceased? Say, in the distance a messenger were to appear, running over the dunes. And say he held a staff aloft. Say the handkerchief that fluttered there were white – if there were wind that day to make it flutter. Would I recognize it as his mark of office? could a truce have been declared? As he approached, say he were to shout something vaguely unintelligible. Would I recognize the password? and how would I respond? would I receive him? would I ask him in? share my meager supper when I have so little for myself? No, no, one can safely count on it; the war will last indefinitely, else why would the redoubt be here? And it is here, make no mistake. Oh, there have been brief disturbances, volleys of gunfire at nightfall, but no sign of the enemy, no visitors of late. No movements, certainly. Only endless days inhabiting the desert, days of the scorpion or of the hawk. On the other hand, standing at attention, sunup to sundown, shackled to the wall, it is not difficult to imagine that time is the enemy, time itself. Each movement, each suggestion of movement subject to doubt. The deprived eye hungering for occurrence. Sunup to sundown. The mind pleading for the unexplained event, seeking to magnify all possible implications. A trickle of sand, say, observed in a hollow between dunes, perhaps a million grains of sand, perhaps a million million, and yet, in the event itself, the avalanche of sand, one might almost hope to recognize the first telltale sign revealing the presence of the enemy beyond one's limited field of vision – or the hidden stakeout of a scout.

Sometimes I imagine rout. I let myself imagine dust, dust at first, little more than a plume, turning, twisting. Innocent, frivolous even, curling in the sunlight. A filmy thing, swaying this way and that, a dust devil perhaps, swirling, undulating in the desert air. Only dust whirling higher, higher still. Or hear perhaps that distant humming that precedes a swarm of locusts, yet the sky remains cloudless without let-up. Louder now. War cries! Ululations! And now, spilling over the dunes, thousands upon thousands, the terrible desert women, their flounces ablaze. Scarlet, carmine and vermilion, sweeping over the dunes, rattling their terrible bone sacks. Chatter of knucklebone, vertebrae, dismembered hooves of the small, swift desert antelope, louder, louder still. I imagine wave upon wave of them, their bodies streaming. Flash of arrows, silver in sunlight. Too blinding, too quick to die of it. Is this how it will end? The wave of red bursting in the throat, choking in the tide of one's own blood. Not like bleeding. No. Nothing like slow bleeding.

Vigilance. Constant vigilance is the daily rule on the frontier. There have been moments of late, dust storms, for example, when the sky becomes occluded with a powder so fine, composed of particles so infinitesimal, the air appears to breathe, as if it could expand, contract, a golden mist where nothing is discernible. A man, say, at ten paces would be indistinguishable. The sun hangs impotent in the low horizon, of no more significance than a tarnished coin. Only by lowering the loophole hatches (there are two) is it possible to wage even what losing battle there is against the dust. Yet raise the binoculars however much I will, stand pressed to the wall, as close to the opening as is ultimately possible, scrutinize the landscape without let-up till the eye rebels and sets up a dancing of its own, there is no sign. Were there movements, would I not detect columns of dust rising, trails of sand lifting in the wake, say, of vehicles struggling over the dunes? There are none. Or evidence now and again of heavy ordnance abandoned or destroyed, or artillery left, charred and gutted in the desert? There is none. Even now certain hills must be riddled with earthworks, mazes of tunnel works, or dugouts. Trenches, lines of defense, redoubts, no doubt other redoubts, perhaps identical or nearly identical to this one. There is nothing. Not a day goes by without raising the binoculars, keeping the lenses free of dust, readjusting the angle of rivalry a hundred times, a hundred hundred times each day. Yet sweep these dunes as I am wont to do, sweep them over one hundred times, one hundred hundred times over, till the eyes refuse, till the ducts tear over, till the mind itself rebels, there is nothing, nothing remotely to suggest, no evidence whatever to support the presence of the enemy. And yet . . . and yet . . . he must be there. Why else would the redoubt be here? That is the obvious thing, of course. And the redoubt is here, make no mistake. If I stand pressed up against the wall, the loopholes allow me ten, say fifteen degrees, fifteen degrees of parched horizon – a strip of time, a slice of light. I call it Day. I wonder. Perhaps somewhere there are redoubts of alternate design with loopholes which admit as many as twenty, or perhaps even twenty-five degrees. What would I call day then? As it stands, I am forced to strain to see, however close I press my eyes to the eyepiece. I force myself from crying out. Outside the dunes lie trembling, stung in shimmery light. Sometimes encroaching, sometimes retreating. I want to shout, *Hold still. Hold still, if only for a moment, long enough for me to take my bearings, before once more taking up your fevered play.* The rocks, the hills, the hollows swim. The very air appears to oscillate in measured beats, to pulse, a scintillate thing.

From within, I watch. I have what weapons I need: compass, sextant, chart box. Detailed maps displaying latitude, longitude and topological formations. All around lies hostile territory. I take my readings, make entries in the logbook. I know exactly where I stand. Chained to the wall. In a dugout of reinforced concrete, with footings sunk in sand – a central point, from which all points radiate.

Sometimes, for one syncopic moment I imagine it could dance, wrench itself free of its moorings, join the fevered movements of the air, swirl in drunken excess with the light, lose its senses utterly. It is not always easy to part the mirage from the real. Not always. Or in another way of speaking, the real from the merely imaginary. And who hungers for such things anyway when they bring a stinging to the eye? At least in that respect, the desert is good. It sucks up unnecessary moisture. Every moment counts. Too hot to dream. I am grateful. The leg irons secure my position, come what may, keep me firmly rooted to my ground. And yet . . . and yet . . . there is a kind of slumber, a breed of forgetfulness, as if memory itself dried up with the stream beds. Caked over and forgot the sea. That is my greatest caution, that in such a moment, loosed from my moorings, the enemy might appear. Perverse thought. The mind's slumber, out of place, suspended, unprodded by the dread of time, time unarmed, shorn of any bearings, with nothing to remind. No dailiness, no going about one's business. Nothing like domestic living.

Or perhaps I am mistaken. Perhaps the redoubt occupies the first line of defense, the in-most line, the very first perimeter, closest to the Capital while all the while I mistakenly supposed it guarded the frontier. Perhaps for this reason the enemy is absent. Can it be it is the Capital I guard, one unit among the many thousands that must ring the Capital? No way of telling. No matter. In the relative scheme of things, in the long view at any rate, frontier or Capital, it is the Capital I guard. I am grateful. There have been no signs of the enemy, no visitors. It has been calm, calm without let-up – except for the occasional volley at sunset. I remain fixed at my post, maintain my vigilance day after day, press the binoculars to my eyes. Oh, there are distractions, momentary lapses, momentary at most. The air shimmers. The vision tires. Sometimes there is a closing of the eyes. Only for a moment. I almost never dream.

The woman that time?

The woman, crouched between the oarlocks, the boat riding at anchor, a momentary lapse, merely momentary. In the endless days which pass without event, the keenest vigilance is required. Not every day is marked by its trickle of sand, or the lengthening of a shadow, observed, or unobserved. The days here pass without a murmur. Sunup to sundown, one day succeeds another. The hour, the light of the sun, the weight of the air, the movement of the wind, all, all are predictable or very nearly predictable. At nine a bird will sing, perched on a branch of creosote. At noon, a dune will have allowed the heat to begin its work. There will be a trickle of sand. By four, the desert has begun to stir, making preparations for the night. A wind will come up, a breeze at first, a sighing of the air currents, barely noticeable. By six, it comes roaring through the loopholes, whistling against the knife sharp ridges of the hatches. The dunes will boil up, the dust, like as not, obscure the sun. I will be forced to lower the mechanism against the suffocation of the sand. I will unlock the leg irons, light the lamp. Place the key once more in one pocket or another where I can pass the time fumbling for it on the morrow. Open the field commander's desk, unclasp the log, flip open the pages, run my index over the findings, every one the same, the same or very nearly. One reading succeeds another. Temperature; wind velocity; relative humidity (there is hardly any – not quantifiable at any rate), and in the box labeled

Observable Phenomena repeat once more: '*at nine a thrush perches on the thorn tree, at noon the dunes begin a stirring as they turn over in their sleep*' (for they sleep by day and labor in the night), '*at four the wind sets up a soft soughing. By nightfall I will have to secure the loophole hatches against the roar.*'

Not every day is redeemed by some event. It is the rare day the wheeling hawk comes to fasten itself, even for an instant, at the corner of my vision, poised weightless, wings spread, riding the air currents. Hawk, sunlight, the soft air are sign enough. On that day, I lower the mechanism quickly, abort the moment when the hawk detaches itself from view, resumes its hunt. And vanishes.

II.

redoute (Fr.) (rədut′) *n.f.*, Redoubt; dancing room.

There is no way, no way to plot these days without measure. In theory, yes. I have everything required. There are banks of files, of camouflage drab, small drawer units (stacked one upon the other for a quick evacuation should the need arise) each subject indexed. Cross-referenced by category. Weather, for example. All notation of the passage of time, of the density of light. Of the velocity of wind currents. Barometric pressure. All these are noted, with particular attention to the unusual occurrence. Wind storms. Sand storms of exceptional severity. Freezing temperatures. Deluge. Troop movements. Delivery of ordnance. Many such files have scant notations – at least as yet – some none at all.

Although my observations are far from complete, each day is separately catalogued, each entry ticked off, item by item, entered in the logbook. In the margin, there appears an uninterrupted flow of ticks to insure that no material is lost, or misplaced – which is as good as lost. Everything in order. Nothing left to chance or to the chance occurrence. I have catalogued extensive data, made a complete inventory, listing every item. Assigned each entry its own catalogue number, including the files themselves, and each folder of files, each one of them cross-referenced by catalogue number.

It has taken up time. Required constant diligence, especially in these days without measure, without the singular event to mark the lapse of time, the passage of the seasons. True, I have everything I need, compass, sextant, quadrant, but without coordinates? With a mere fifteen-degree slice of the night sky, if there are stars, the loopholes are placed too low to see them. With so little to guide me, time, and place are lost, or at the very least misplaced. There is nothing and next to nothing. More and more I shun the light, make a practice of the darkness. I lower the loophole hatches (there are two). Extinguish the light. Fold my body inside the sleepsack. Listen to my ankle hum where, all day long, the leg iron has chafed it. A throb, a comfortable pain. A threshold pain. I call it Living. A reminder, yes. Not so severe I cannot rest. Not so intense I cannot sleep.

The heat of the day must take its toll. Sleep must come quickly to those who live out their days in the desert. When the shackles are unlocked, when day slips from my ankles, I am free to roam, float in the envelope in which I breathe, listen to the drumming in the ears. A hum, a nudge, a fold of time. Always it astonishes me, the drumming in the night that tells me I am here, it is now, not then, not dawn, but now. Stuck in the web.

I rarely dream. And yet, and yet. . . . There is a sense. I have the sense I am visited. In some dark stain of light, a presence dwells, huge, hirsute and corporeal, moving things about, arranging things. Things that fit or do not fit. Bent over the drawing board, drafting, susurrus of pen on paper, charting, plotting. Recording. Wind currents, the movement of waters, the sways of light, tearing off sheet after sheet, letting each leaf fall whispering to the ground while all the while I crouch in darkness, scratching like a dog to be let in. Pleading. *I am the spirit of your employment.* A child's voice. Mine? Mine, then? Or some woman's. But the titan persists undeterred. I wring my hands, clutch my wrist, my fingers overlap. Third finger bypasses tip of thumb. Thin. Thinner by far than ever I imagined. My wrist? Mine, certainly, but with room to spare. Can it be another body I inhabit, one grown thin and strange to me?

That whispering of paper, that rustling as of something sliding through the chute, what possible explanation? Throw off the sleepsack, let my feet drop to the ground. Light the lamp. An envelope has fallen from the chute. An envelope bordered in black. A letter? A letter perhaps. I make out the word *cancelled. . . .* It must be the odd postman who ventures this far in uncharted territory with no road or track to guide him. I want to call out. I hurl my weight against the mechanism. The hatches squeal open. But there is no one. The night is empty. From somewhere moonlight sweeps the dunes in its deadly pewter light. A blurring of wings fans the air against my ear. A bat, perhaps, come to keep me company. I shut the loopholes once more to keep the poison of the night air out.

The envelope feels pulpy to the touch – like butcher's paper. The seal has come open. I slip the letter out. I hold it under the lamp to read. *You never noticed anything. Now look: look what happened while you slept.* A photograph falls to the ground. Under the lamp's dim glow I examine what first I take to be a quarry, deep as a mountain in reverse. Red earth, ocher. Ponds where the ground water has accumulated. In the far distance, fully clothed, a woman bathes. Who? Who might she be? Or perhaps she is merely stooping in the water. Washing or examining something. Either way, impossible to tell what she is doing. Or who she is. Yet she is there. In the foreground there is a ramp. A series of sieve boxes clutters the roadway. There is a scattering of men here and there, but none seems to be working. A cloud of blue exhaust fumes curls out of the lower right-hand corner. A diesel truck must rev its motor some place in the foreground, out of sight.

The paper unfolds like an accordion. Fallen open, the image seems not quite the same. Not quite the quarry I had thought. The same great stretch of ground, yes, but now the sun is absent. A wind seems to blow out of the north. Here and there, someone strides briskly, collar turned up against the cold. Great pits have been excavated, trucks wait to be loaded with topsoil, and in the far distance, dead branches sprawl over dead ground. Yet when I look closer, what I first took to be tundra becomes a bramble of wooden chairs, thousands of them. Thousands upon thousands. Theater chairs. They lie abandoned, but in a desert where there is no sun to bleach them white.

The recess of the envelope conceals another photograph. A woman's figure. Lying in a bank of roses and relatives, all standing respectfully, hats held in work-gnarled hands. Candles burning everywhere. And she – can it be? – it appears to be my mother lying there. Quite recognizably my mother. And yet . . . I scan the address. Campin. Gulen. Gulen Campin. And the postmark: XII. xxi. XXI. Another time – or century perhaps – and yet, without mistake, the image is my mother's. Curious. Who can have sent this letter? with this unsettling photograph? Or perhaps it was the wind. Perhaps the envelope has lain all this while in the crevice of the mail chute, which I, so certain no message would ever come, neglected to open until now. Yet unmistakably it is my mother, lying on her bier, her face a plaster death mask, her thick-soled theater shoes clearly visible, her pipe still hanging at the corner of her mouth. From time to time – as if in life – the bowl lights up, some master undertaker's touch. One of the company coughs discreetly and hides his embarrassment behind his hat.

Handwriting slants across the page. *We had to bury everything, her clothes, her household goods, even the goat. Nothing was left. We arranged everything ourselves. The rites. Disposal of the body. . . . Look what happened while you slept.* A contentious sentiment without a doubt, but hardly meant for me. An artifact, this letter, from another century. Of value to someone once, perhaps, but now of use to no one – not me in any case. And yet the photograph is of my mother. Or of what may once have been my mother. I let it flutter to the ground.

In my hands the accordion falls open completely. The last fold shows the day becoming darker. Or perhaps the pits have become deeper. As if the houses no longer rose so much as sank – or at least they seem to sink. And yet the signs are not so readily apparent. A subtle change of light, of season, perhaps, and the alleys become obscured, the streets somber, inimical thoroughfares. I follow the fellow walking, collar turned up against the chill. Just now, squatting closer to see, he notices a thin line, a crack which has only now appeared, a tiny fissure where the foundation of a house parts company with the ground. Benign, hardly worth notice. And the man in any case must pass quickly, his collar turned up against the cold, muffling his face, obstructing his view. Probably he thinks only of the cold – if he thinks at all – of its icy talons prying up his sleeves. Or he thinks of gaining warmth or shelter, of a room perhaps, or a corner of a room, a place as close as possible to the fire – if there is wood to make a fire. His attention is turned elsewhere. It may be some time before some fellow townsman notices the crack. Perhaps it will have gaped only a little wider. Or it will have yawned a little deeper. Perhaps it will have to become a crevice before some housewife emerging at first light to scrape her sewer clear of offal will allow her distracted eye to wander long enough to notice the ground come quite undone, the house left stranded in the air. She will call out to her husband, *Zog, Zog, come see. . . .* In her confusion, she will drop the scraper, abandoning it on the paving stones where it will have fallen with a clatter. Inside, in the dark she will shake her unsuspecting husband, still besotted in his drunken sleep (having pissed himself in bed). She will shout at the top of her fishwifely lungs, *Zog! Zog, wake up! The house has come unstuck from the ground!* And he, waking reluctantly, will pile abuse on her till it fairly bows her head. And she not letting up for an instant, *Come see, come say for yourself if I lie.*

But Zog sleeps. He pulls the ragged covers (former grain sacks probably) higher, burying his head. Until the day perhaps when, stumbling down his front stairs at dusk on his way to the tavern, he trips on the bottom step and goes sprawling into air. And sees how his stoop now soars, cantilevered above the roadbed, and how the ground beneath it gapes, and returns raging to his wife. *Elup! Imbecile woman, it is the world, you fool! The world has come unstuck from the house!*

A photograph without commentary in any case, perhaps the tacit record of a subsiding city, where the huts have remained fixed, stone upon stone, the ladders in place, the cupboards undisturbed, but where houses grew taller, stretched into buildings, buildings gave birth to skylines, roadways appeared, ribbons of asphalt spread over the landscape, bridges gave rise to cities of dream, but where less and less there was ground, less and less there was room. Where the time came when sealing the streets became a necessity, when the councilors moved to lock the gates, where the walls had become full to bursting, but prey no more, never prey. Not to attack, or to contamination from without, immune to decay from within, but where more and more the inhabitants lost ground, sealed in the glassy perfection of their floating walls, and nothing changed but for this one thing, no stopping it, no reversing the trend, this slow subsidence of ground, this gradual floating in the air. And if for a moment some maverick wind snatched an unruly hat off someone's head in some dark alley, or raised an unsuspecting skirt, the courts were there to fix the blame, mete out penalties, see to it that no wind raged, no whirlwinds ever disturbed the clean perfection of those sunken streets, all quiet (excepting when the freak winds rage), and silent as a photograph.

There is more. One last page. The postscript reads, *Still wriggling on your tightrope, are you? hovering some place up there? Well, well. At least you aren't dead! Still hanging by a thread! There you are, spidery aerialist, come separated from your kind, dangling precariously, kicking and flailing over your self-appointed void, alone on the frontier as you 'keep watch', as you 'stand guard', as you 'monitor' the shifting sands at the margins of the world. Tell me, who will be there when the body exerts its fearful tyrannies? And when it betrays you altogether at the last, who will hold the basin? wash the bedpan out, send you to your resting place?*

We're not going to wake you. Oh, no, don't wake! You'll surely fall. With no one left to catch the echoes of your disappearing cry. No signature of any kind. There must be some mistake. An envelope, addressed to someone who may have occupied the fort, someone probably before myself, someone other than myself. Someone named Gulen. A man's name.

Or a woman's perhaps?

No matter. No one comes to mind. Poor Gulen. I try to imagine who he (or she) may have been. Such wretched tidings. Enough to make one lie awake at night, unable to sleep, dreaming of butcher paper and collapse. Imagine the relatives, holding vigil by Gulen's mother through the night. Sharing her last moments as she balances between life and death, still juggling (for the benefit of the clergy) now one baby sin, now another, sins of omission, sins of contrition, still doubled up in convulsive laughter, spinning out all the little chubby-fingered, peckerdildo children she might have bothered to conceive if only her trashy clown's motley hadn't gotten in the way – sharing their stale sweat, arguing all night *soto voce* before sending the absent Gulen a final ultimatum.

TAKING DRASTIC MEASURES MAKE MOTHER STOP LONG ENOUGH TO BURY STOP COME HOME AT ONCE STOP

Poor Gulen. Poor, hapless Gulen. The postman may not have bothered poking the notice far enough down the chute, or Gulen may have had a bad night, or he (or she) may never have existed, or he (or she) may have read the message in 1942, long after his (or her) mother died, or he (or she) may have had dyspepsia from eating too much chocolate, or the relatives couldn't decide whether to let the mortician lay his (or her) mother out in her wedding dress, (all lacy virginal extravagance) or her clown's motley, or stitch a shroud for her combining elements of both.

She may have died never having received Gulen's goodbye or given him (or her) her blessing? She may have. Or the relatives may have failed to observe a decent interval of mourning or veil themselves in black. They may have. What if Gulen's absence allowed them to give vent at last to the frustration and disappointment they surely must have felt. It may have. What if they had to brave the crossfire of rebel snipers all the way to the cemetery, braying at the top of their lungs, singing one ill-mannered dirge after another?

Gulen, Gulen, bastard child, **(chwang, chwang)**
Born of woman who wouldn't die, **(ZZZing)**
Thumbed her nose as she lay in state. **(fwang,fwang)**
  She could never keep a mate.
I weep for you, I weep, Gulen, **(chow, chow, chow)**
Your fate is not quite human: **(djjjing)**
You will never be a proper man, **(ching,ching,ching)**
  And can't learn to be a woman. **(pause to reload)**
  I weep for you, I weep, Gulen, **(etc. etc. etc.)**

They may have, and because Gulen made the relatives wait an eternity for his (or her) reply, they may have been forced to stall for time, singing all the etceteras all the way to the cemetery – pitiful doggerel, in any case – and by the time they reached the grave site they may have all been shot, every one of them – except for Gulen's mother who was probably still laughing. Why? Because, unbeknownst to them, the straight jacket the relatives finally picked out for her shroud was bullet proof.

All very nice, this noodling. But suppose Gulen had never recognized a mother? Say, unlike most, he (or she) was raised by two grandmothers, one a solid citizen, the other a dizzy beauty. One (the redhead) wore black velvet. The other (the brunette) wore frilly lace froufrous. The redhead tied a velvet ribbon round her neck. The brunette wore a lacy picture hat. The redhead designed precision chronometers while hatching thirteen children. The brunette – regrettably – went mad. But Gulen couldn't bring him(or her)self to attend the funeral because he (or she) didn't exactly know which one of the two grandmothers had died, the starchy one who was always squinting through her watchmaker's glass, or the *bonne vivante* who forgot to arrange for dinner, but who always kept chocolate truffles in her bustier to guard against emergencies.

An amusing gloss, although, come to think of it, there may be another, somewhat more somber explanation: Gulen's grandmothers, for various, mutually compelling reasons (unknown at first to Gulen, unknown equally – as it will eventually be revealed – to the grandmothers) lived in the same house, thereby sparing Gulen the painful task of deciding which one he (or she) preferred to live with, or the onus whenever he wished to visit of always having to run back and forth between them. The chronometer grandmother refused to let Gulen play cards on Sundays, but the chocolate grandmother reassured Gulen when he (or she) grew up he (or she) wouldn't necessarily have to remain a saint. The grandmothers died. When the morticians came with their dressmaker's dummies and their black plastic garbage bags, the relatives demanded bills of lading before letting them load the defuncti on their undertakers' wagons. That's when they discovered that all along the chocolate grandmother had really been a man. That version is a little more uncomfortable. But there is yet another interpretation, this one a little more perverse: Gulen's grandmothers were really Gulen's mother and father. Or, most sinister of all, vice versa. Conceivably there could be no end to the Waltz of the Grandmothers. The steps! The variations! The damaged genealogy. The bizarre twists and turns!

A contemptible story at best. Without the slightest merit. A diversionary pastime, and in any case, involving someone other than myself. No matter how brief the lapse, there is hardly time for such frivolity. Domestic disarray may have its place, but not on the frontier. The march of events is inexorable. Barely a moment of inattention, or a fraction of a moment, and already the desert may lie gasping, stunned by heat. There is no telling what may have occurred. This kind of falling off of attention is a rare thing, an exceedingly rare thing with me. Nothing for it now but to douse the lamp. Open the hatch covers (there are two), search my pockets for the key. Fumble – always fumble – with the leg iron. Hasten to take up my position. Ready the binoculars, adjust the angle of rivalry. Train them on the distant slopes. The sun has already risen nearly thirty degrees. The thorn tree is bare, the thrush has flown, but evidently not yet quite so far that one of its branches can't still reverberate slightly, a silent testament to its absent weight.

III.

redoubt (rĭ-dout´) *n.*, A defensive fortification placed within a permanent rampart; a work placed within an outwork.

There are days here, weeks possibly, that seem to pass without distress. Perhaps not so much distress as anxiety, although were I pressed to describe them, these lulls, what would I say? That someone (or something) *other than myself* were present here, in these confines? A presence in the presence of my presence? I cannot say. Why would there be this question of presence in absence, or absence in presence? Impossible to tell. Perhaps that is not it. Perhaps it is a presence, an actual presence. Or is it merely an absence, the absence (or presence) of anguish? As if someone were present? There is a distinction. Presence or absence. Presence in absence. Or the presence of anguish unrecognized, and when it comes calling, crouching at the oarsman's bench, letting the oars rest idle in the oarlocks, might it wear the dress of anguish (if anguish could be said to wear a dress?)

– *Where are you going?* If I listen I can still hear the wash of water, lapping against the pilings. A woman's voice. Mine? Mine, then? Yet it is a woman I hear. Anguish? Not exactly. More like absence. That time – before waking – that time I found myself entangled, fumbling in the sleepsack, and brushed against the swell of breast . . . troubling? In the normal sense? Perhaps not so much troubling. I remember my actual thought was of amusement. Imagine! A woman. Here. On the frontier, manning the redoubt. Shackling herself by day – when the loopholes are ajar – forced to hold her ground, prepared to defend against all circumstance. Conducting experiments, taking measurements, cross-referencing. recording observations in the logbook, examining the readings. Ascribing dates and times to things.

Sometimes I dream of throwing off the bedclothes, exulting in the shudder of my thighs, blue in moonlight, as if wavering underwater. Always I start in surprise to find my body cleft, seeing the dark fruit that, even asleep, promises sweetness to the traveler. And touch. And touch, that soft place – say it – island of wet in the dryness, island of soft in the darkness. Ah, then, yes: the place of refuge, home of consolation, yes.

But war is not a place for women. Rigor, rigor is the first defense against vagueness, and the things of vagueness. Here, where the days pass without measure, void of event, there must be constant vigilance. Measures must be taken. Consciously taken. Nothing must be left to chance or to the chance occurrence. Hostilities must be declared against vagueness, all that is dreaming, undeclared. Always the outside must command my full attention. Gathering data, recording my entries, updating the logbook. The redoubt is at best a vehicle, a storage place for the instruments, the chart box, the files, and ultimately, for its occupant, a shell of no intrinsic consequence other than the fulfillment of certain functions. Gathering data, for example. Defending against the enemy. Consider. Have I perhaps grown overly accustomed to the occupant? Might there have been a time, a time – even now perhaps – when the eye was present here but in another form? Consider that.

Position: *curled.*
Hair: *sparse or balding.*
Lids: *open; at other times shut.*
Build (for purposes of identification in the absence of dental charts): *undifferentiated.*
Bones: *not applicable.* (Not yet.)

Consider: wrists? Ankles? Impossible to say. Not yet. Unable to place a name on them exactly. I confess: in the bunk from time to time, on awaking, or before extinguishing the lamp, I allow my legs to dangle over the edge. I do this in the full knowledge that I am unobserved. I let them dangle over the edge. Always it surprises me, the frailty of legs. Can they be mine, I ask myself? when they might very well belong to another, a frail hemophiliac boy, perhaps, or a girl surprised in her first menarche (the dark welling). Images come. Intimations of another life: train depots, marching bands, and guard dogs straining at the leash. So many legs left dangling from so many bunks, their owners unable to rouse themselves, to touch the ground, to imagine day.

Circumstance. All this of little consequence in the indifferent scheme of things. I am here. For the moment. Here and not elsewhere. Who I am and not another. And yet, and yet . . . I see myself clearly: the sickbed, the bloodied sheet, hand pressed to groin, stanching the wound.

It is better, far better in the desert where the sand lies dormant in the sunlight. Where there is nothing and next to nothing to remind. True, one must maintain a certain vigilance, a certain defense, against darkness and the things of darkness. There are tasks to be completed, schedules to uphold. In principle (but for the enemy) I am free to roam. I could, for example, walk out onto the sands, cross the hollows, trudge over the dunes, scale distant scarps perhaps. There is still equipment here, ice axes, crampons, pitons. Rope left over from another time. I imagine my footfalls pressing over the sands, sinking past the ankle, the white heat, the blinding light to realize that leaving is impossible.

Sometimes I come back to it, between lowering the binoculars and taking up the charts, or stowing the sleepsack and fastening the leg irons – in moments between moments – : my legs dangling over the bunk. Curious. As if something were nudging at my elbow, the dog or cat of memory angling for scraps. Sometimes one catches sight of certain things years afterwards. Things etched, burned in the eyes if abandoned in the memory. Sometimes I see them, more or less. Or Gulen's mother (or my mother perhaps?) falling that time on Theater

Street under the stampeding hooves of horses, her red hair going white with shock weeks afterwards.

Irrelevant thoughts. Of use to no one. Pry open the logbook. Decide between the sharpened pencil or the pen. Time to declare hostilities against vagueness, to enter the reverse notations of the late afternoon, waning of sunlight, waxing of wind, ensure that nothing is left to chance. Review the findings in the logbook. Trace them (if there is any question) first in pencil. Lightly. Trace them (if necessary) to permit erasure before entering them with any permanence. Erase the lapse, the temporary lowering of the lids, the momentary truce. Correct the swimming of the figures on the page. Cover an incidental faltering – the closing of the eyes – before entering the findings with steely permanence. Latitude in the latitude column, longitude in the longitude column, carefully tabulated, true within the hour, minute, second. Painstakingly inking in the findings one by one: here abscissa, there ordinate. The regular routine. Without deviation. Without indulgence. The fixed point. Maintain the frontiers, lines, vectors – all fixed quanta in a sea of change. All in its place. A little calligraphic excursion now and again, room for the frivolous deviation from time to time, but otherwise regular. Fixed. Secure. Better that way. Time to calibrate the chronometer tomorrow, time enough then. Tonight, tick off the findings, enter in the log, cross-reference by category, stack the file boxes for quick retrieval should the need arise.

In the night I dream of flood. Far below, a gang of masons is at work, stirring quicklime in a vat; teams of draft animals labor under the yolk. In little more than a moment, towers rise up, vast cities of water, lashing the shore, uprooting great rocks, burying the gang of masons writhing in their own quicklime, swamping them like corks bobbing on the surface of the water, strewing boulders in their wake. Cries in the distance, distress of the drowning, of the doomed before burial. Yet at this distance, their screams come as some distant flapping of wings or the groans of someone turning over in his sleep. Can it be my own awakening cry? I throw off the sleepsack, strain against the weight of the mechanism. The hatches squeal open. A crow flaps its startled wings and caws into the morning. I watch it rising, fanning the air, smaller, smaller, smaller yet until it becomes a speck, barely distinguishable, and melts into the air. The dunes lie still, maintaining their pretense. Advancing, retreating. The day takes hold. Brush away the darkness, fasten the leg irons. Swing the binoculars free. Raise them to the eye. I can see it at first glance: the dunes have crept closer, imperceptibly to the untrained eye perhaps (for the dunes sleep by day, in the night they labor). Here one has mounded slightly, while closeby another sinks. From one day to another their sway is almost never the same. Mornings it astounds me: the outside appears newly made while inside, dark things team with wretched life, laying their eggs of memory whether one wills or no, hatching their spurred, horned creatures, clinging to the walls, lumbering on stumpy legs, armies of disgust, bivouacked in tents of sticky filament, overrun by nymphs, millions of them. Food for bats.

I let the eyepiece scan the horizon, edging slowly along wave after wave of rise and fall. Sine and cos. Sand. Stillness. No fluttering of wings. Even the wind is absent. The day's still point. Quiet. Something to be said for it. Poised on the frontier (uncertain which). Dreaming. Caught between definitions. I call it Living. Here. Not there.

Wanting?

No. Not exactly wanting. Why? When I have everything required, compass, sextant, chronometer. And leg irons to chafe against my ankles. Not a burdensome reminder in any case. I have merely to readjust my position. An improvement, certainly. Not much perhaps, but enough, in the relative scheme of things, to minimize conscious discomfort.

Already the heat has begun to rise. I train the binoculars. Waves of captive air shimmer over the surface of the dunes. As far as the eye can reach, everything begins to scintillate. The sky gives no quarter, already white with heat. A city rises. Huts grow to buildings, buildings form skylines. Nothing new, certainly. Nothing out of the ordinary. Merely the stuff of which mirage is made. A momentary trembling. A shimmering. A temporary oscillation of the light. Fully explainable. A common optical phenomenon. Reflection. Refraction. Nothing unusual. Nothing to write home about in any case.

In the great distance, a sand plume rises up. A temporary aberration of the light? No. Too close to the surface. The wind. The wind, perhaps, toying with the sand. Flushing out a flock of crows. Grazing one crest of dune and now another. A puff of wind. Raising a column of dust. A temporary phenomenon. Nothing worthy of note. A kind of spume on the horizon. Distinct. A kind of spray. A spray of wind. A jet. Curious. Something there. Unusual? Yet the air is calm, without perceptible movement. Perhaps not wind. Probably not. And yet . . . something there. A puff. A flaring up. A dust devil, perhaps, making mock of the horizon. Recurring. Replicable. Now rising, now falling. A wave. There and not there. There and there again. Repeating itself. Something. Distinct. There and not there. Present. Absent. Present once more. Endless series of repetitions. Describe:

Frequency: *recurring, every second or so. Or fraction of a second.*

Amplitude: At this distance? Impossible to tell. A speck, no bigger than a gnat. What? Gone? Something and now nothing. Wipe the eyepiece. Raise the binoculars. Scan the horizon. A thorough sweep. Comb the mass of distant dunes. Vanished. Gone. No sign in any case.

And now again! A distant flaring up. A microscopic burst. Lower, lower yet, as if the wind were needling the sand, fanning up wave after wave of sandspray. An insect. Describe. A speck no bigger than a gnat . . . two! Two now, running, running on the far horizon, scrambling, throwing up bursts of sandspray in their wake. Clearly see them now careening over the dunes: two arms, two legs, running, running down the flank of a distant dune, kicking up sand, one running, one stumbling. Appearing, disappearing. Now reappearing. Randomly, perhaps. A summer outing? Or is A pursuing T? (Or T evading A?) Or perhaps T and A are but the secondary manifestation of primary phenomena. For example, C (not yet within sight) could be pursuing A, who is pursuing T. Or G (still farther afield) could be pursuing J (still out of sight) who is pursuing C, who is pursuing A. Or G *and* J could be pursuing C (just out of view) who is pursuing A, who is pursuing T. Or perhaps in reality A is running away from G, and his (or her) evasive actions trigger J who pursues C, unaware that G is bringing up the rear. Endless possibilities! Permutations, combinations. Simple equations. Binomials, quadratics, simple curves, compound curves, complex curves, compound-complex curves, one after another, pretexts for endless speculation, to wit: why are they all running? what are they running toward? Where are they running from? And can it be that their unforeseen appearance is but a titillating prelude to more rosy things to come? Certainly a rare occurrence, when there have been so few visitors of late, none to write home about in any case.

There again. Someone running: a woman, bright red hair! A woman running, stumbling. Running, scrambling, stumbling. And now that other, cresting the dune. Some thing, some weapon held aloft. A baton, perhaps, a staff of office! A staff of office, certainly, a staff of office held aloft. And something fluttering there: white! A messenger! (is the war over?) a messenger, bearing the white handkerchief of truce! Closer, ever closer. A messenger, it must be. But gaining, gaining on that other. And she, running, stumbling, switching direction. And he, in close pursuit, gaining, always gaining on her. And she, a distraction perhaps, perverting the commission of his office, running, still running, stumbling, rising now over the crest, disappearing in its trough and he about to catch up to her, staff of office still held high. Screams in the distance. Screams of distress? Rape! Rape? An interference. Can it be? Strange visitors, certainly. Or perhaps screams of satisfaction, yes, why not? *Do it to me, stick it to me, Charlie. Give me the business.* Yes, why not? No truce just yet.

Vanished. No trace. Not there. Not there at all. Silence. Lower the binoculars. Wipe the eyepiece clean of sweat. Readjust the angle of rivalry, steady my grip. Scan the horizon. Keep the miserable objective in some kind of focus. Drop lower, higher, lower yet. No trace. Nothing. Come and gone. Imagined for all I know – or dreamed – but for footprints here and there, soon to be smoothed over by the wind and swept away without a trace. A mere fluctuation of the landscape. A temporary disturbance perhaps. Temporary at best. A momentary turbulence in the scintillation of the light. A flurry in the overall stillness of the air. Hardly remarkable. Hardly noteworthy even, let alone a prelude to more promising things to come. Certainly not visitors, thank goodness no visitors! There is not even a heading for Visitors, not yet! Nothing like visitors. And who would come here after all? There is no road. The wind has covered all traces. Perhaps there was a track that led here once. There may have been a track by now quite blown over.

Picture it! A world freed once more of event! No traces, no frivolities. Only endless days in the desert. The scorpion, and the hawk from time to time. Shifting sands. The redoubt, fixed at last. Perhaps the sole fixed point in a sea of change. True, the sand invades. Everywhere there is dust. The desert displays annoying dynamisms while within, within my entries multiply. The files proliferate. Already they have come to occupy an entire wall – the north wall (to be precise) wherein each event, each observation – since my coming – is carefully recorded, allotted its required space. Given its due weight, no less, no more.

Taking stock of the file boxes stacked against the wall – merely looking at them – is a calming thing. Camouflage drab, yes, but visible. Fixed, quantifiable. And yet . . . and yet, data expands. Accumulates. The drawers will fill. Overnight they appear to grow. A time will doubtless come when they will bulge to overflowing. A time when I shall have to apply my full weight to force them shut. What then? If there is still more data? What then? Though I strive for brevity, make do with less, less time, less space, nothing rests. Nothing is complete. Perhaps it is entropy which is the enemy. The restlessness of things. It, too, is an encroachment, but of another kind. An invasion – like the dunes – against which I can do nothing or next to nothing.

It could go on. It could go on like this. Indefinitely, perhaps. I could scan the distant slopes. Take my readings, record my findings in the logbook. Reference and cross reference. . . . Futility? In the long run? Not necessarily. Not necessarily. There is no telling. No telling, for example, when or under what conditions the enemy might appear. Certainly no one has come of late, at least no one to write home about – with two negligible exceptions. But signs of the enemy? Hardly. A warning, perhaps. A mere warning of possible things to come. Of what? By whom? Too soon to tell. And now? No sign. No trace in any case. Not at this remove. No indication of any passage. Nothing. Raise the binoculars. Sweep the dunes.

Backward and forward. Higher. Higher yet. Nothing. Tracks in the sand? At this remove nothing. Not with this power at any rate. A rare occurrence, no doubt. Unusual. Trick of the landscape, mirage, perhaps, aberration of the light. Call it temporary relief. Or hallucination? Hardly. Yet those screams. More than passing evidence, or lapse of landscape? Momentary? Merely momentary? Or a trick of the lens perhaps. A momentary diversion. A local excitation: dawn of an event, anticipation of things to come . . . and now? Now what? Ah, yes: letdown, the solitary monster. Familiar. There-and-not-there. There by absence, by present emptiness.

IV.

redoubt (rĭ-dout´) *v.t.*, To doubt, to dread.

It has been calm – too calm – for many days. I scan the horizon. Through the eyepiece, everywhere, over every dune, the frantic air appears to tremble. The desert lies baking, stunned by sunlight, shimmering, incendiary. I imagine it about to burst into a lake of fire. Yet it is a day, a day like any other. I stand chained to the wall, as I am always chained, training the binoculars along the distant slopes, along what was once a valley floor, flooded once, an inland sea. Water appears for a brief moment, a perfect lens, without bubble or blemish, reflecting the sky's white heat. The sun assaults the distant dunes, causing them to breathe and pucker. The noon hour passes.

I train the eyepiece upward toward the horizon. The desert lies gasping. Inert. I scan the dunes looking for the movement, any movement that will punctuate the general, give it a name. There is none. Adjust the angle of rivalry, train the binoculars. Scan for the solitary invasion on the far horizon. The possible figure(s) skating over the surface of the dunes, running. Running perhaps, stumbling. Regaining balance. Propelling puffs of sandspray in their wake. Running. Where? Destination? Unknown. From whom? undetermined. And why? unexplained. A messenger perhaps, bearing word of truce who may have been distracted from his loftier purpose. Who may have yielded to his baser nature with very little prodding, allowing some wayward Daughter of Eve to pry him loose from his commission. Impossible to say. Or perhaps he set out with his net, innocently hunting butterflies, and succumbed only later to darker, more sinister designs. Greater men have done no less.

And yet . . . and yet . . . those cries. Heard them distinctly, cries of distress in the distance, or cries of concupiscence perhaps – transport even – if one is to believe everything one hears. Can something like an event be said to have occurred? An actual event? Rape? Rape, possibly? or simple fornication? Impossible to know. There would have to exist some kind of proof: a bloody bed sheet; or the severed head of some hapless cock, decapitated – in all likelihood – long past its days of usefulness. No way of telling. And nothing remotely resembling any of the above may actually have occurred. Nothing to explain those apparently random comings and goings, those clumsy runnings and stumblings.

Perhaps seen from another vantage point, such movements may have taken on a far more deliberate aspect, but the rise and fall of intervening dunes may have impaired any attempt at plausible interpretation. Or they may have been entirely devoid of any serious intent, the convulsions of madmen, say, or somnambulists, unrecognized even by themselves. And yet . . . yet . . . they may have indicated something . . . something, or very nearly something. Some purpose, some demonstrable direction, an event perhaps. Possibly even an event. But what kind of event? And without proof, no proof of anything of consequence actually occurring – not in any manner of speaking, at any rate – and with all evidence vanished now, long vanished, nothing to write home about in any case – can an event be said actually to have occurred? Can a plausible description be entered in the logbook? Or included in the files?

Visitors (of late): two. Possibly
Point of origin: unknown
Destination: unconfirmed
Purpose: fornication?

Fornication, or merely copulation? Futility. Futility. Stupid stuff, all this. Of use to no one.

A wind is rising. I raise the binoculars, adjust the eyepiece, wipe the lenses free of dust. Particles begin to swirl, suspended in a spreading cloud of dust until there is little to be seen. Hills, dunes, all vanish, receding depth by depth. The wind sets the loopholes to whistling. The day begins its slow decline. I set down the binoculars. Fumble for the key. Unlock the leg iron. Lower the hatch covers against the gale.

Another day. Light the lamp. Update. Record conditions: visibility clouded, going on obscure. Air velocity: at first tranquil, or within the range of tranquil, growing to gale force. Humidity: risible. Always in the desert: there has been no rain in over one hundred years. Consider. If something happens, is it always a function of perception? For example, unclasping the logbook now, it is apparent the binding has come loose from the end papers at the spine. Nothing dramatic. The sort of thing one has come to expect, the slow accretions of time, or entropy, perhaps. Time past to time present. Time present to time future. The natural revolt of small things. Looking about there are other signs. At the juncture between the sleep loft and the supporting members, a spider web dangles, disinhabited now, host to the dull and broken wings of insect carcasses. Can it be all this happens whether one notices or not?

In the quiet moments, the times of reverie – between the murmur of the air currents in the early afternoon, before the stirring of the dunes at sunset – the general may give way to the particular, if there is some movement, say, if some small desert animal ruffles the surface of a dune, some bird lights on a branch of the tamarisk, causing a momentary trembling, until the branch, disturbed, recovers its apparent equilibrium. The general may yield to the particular. Unmet, the eyes begin to smart, every muscle, every sinew aches.

If one could forget, for a moment at least, forget the sand encroaching, overlook the heat, the sun beating down. Overlook the givens and partly givens, the thing, for example, that causes the dunes to shimmer, one could then allow the eye to seek a landscape of its own: bauxite hills that wind along the edge of distant seas, wetlands lying fallow, host to flocks of snowy water fowl. The eye itself stalls in the presence of sand without limit (and there is more, yet more to come).

I dream of Gulen's mother in the night. Dense banks of flowers, white, or near white (impossible to tell) surrounding her. Long tapers flicker at her head and feet, illuminating the faces of seven mourners who stand to either side, gaunt, grieving, all of them, dwarfed with age, hats held in work-worn hands. The embalmers have not yet done their work: her face is still exposed, but her hands, already bandaged, rest above the satin pall. In death she has become a virgin. A lying-in table waits in a darkened corner of the room. The undertakers position the defunct, raise and open her desiccated legs. From between her frozen thighs, a dark stain oozes. A dog whines and scratches at the door, and behind it, Gulen's father, Campin *pere*, hides, hat in hand, making himself small, a cuckhold in his own house, while one by one, Gulen's seven uncles kiss the pale blue lips of the defunct before passing outside through the darkened corridor.

I wake in darkness. A storm has blown up. The wind shrieks as it cuts its tongue on the blades of the loophole hatches. I lie gasping in my sack, listening to the racing of my blood. If I screamed now, I would not hear it. Not even I. No voice could make itself heard above the roar. Outside the world turns itself inside out, the argument of the elements: hiss of sand, barrage of rocks pelting the redoubt. Yet inside, sufficiently small, I pass without notice. There is some satisfaction in finding oneself small. Curled. Of no more significance than a worm. To rest, held fast in this cyst that is mine and mine alone, cauled in the safety of the fort, rocked in the arms of the whirlwind, impervious to sting of sand, to scream of wind, to shriek of gale. Locked. Safe. Safe, I ask myself? On such a night as this? when I flail in dream, a fish bursting its gills, impaled on the hook of sleep, tongue heaving for water? Submerged in the great dreaming maw – my ocean without end – scaling reefs pocked with eye of eel lurking in the crevices, claw of foot, saw of tooth and spring of tentacle, there to eat, or to be eaten, home to the veiled women streaming over the sands, their shattering cries, their terrible bone sacks. Nothing like slow bleeding – no. Nothing like slow bleeding.

Alarms in the night, distinctly heard them. Barrage of rocks fragmenting against the walls, talons of the wind tearing at the loophole hatches. The stirring of the dunes laboring in darkness (for they sleep by day and labor in the night). When at last morning dawns I ask myself, how can I find it in myself after such a night to stow the sleepsack in the overhead loft, trouble with the mechanism, crank open the hatches, fumble for the key once more, fasten the leg iron, raise the binoculars, adjust the angle of rivalry? Resume the regular routine?

It could go on like this. It could go on indefinitely. No stemming light or stilling time. Day seeps through the crack of the loophole covers. I slide to my feet, lean my weight against the counterweights. The mechanism squeals open. I rub my eyes. Is it possible? The dunes loom closer, pretending innocence, blander than a postcard greeting from the desert: there the brush of creosote, the oriole fastened to its branch, there the trickle of sand arrested. Hollows etched by heat, the sky empty, without measure, no clouds worrying its brow. Still. Frozen. Safer than a photograph. And I. Caught in the mesh. Framed in a stillness that forgot to breathe.

Unknown what is happening to the east of my position, and to some degree to the south and north as well. But to the west the signs are unmistakable. The sand looms closer, ever closer, advancing grain by grain. I have only to verify the angle of slipface to gauge the rate of migration. I raise the binoculars. I compare. Repeated readings confirm it. How could it be otherwise? That is my greatest caution, that after such a night, unvisited by rest, when dawn finds me drained, the blood flushed like sand through an hourglass, the unforeseen occurs. Relax my vigilance once too often, allow the mechanism to rust, or the eye piece to cloud over, even for a moment . . . then what? Invasion? Rout? The mound and sink of terrifying dreams?

The loopholes offer me fifteen degrees, fifteen degrees of the night sky. Hardly wide enough to recognize the Dog Star or greet Arcturus with his train. Caution is the rule on the frontier. Stealth, and stealth only is the order of the night. How to stop the door of dream long enough to take my bearings. Wait for the evening winds to calm, for the golden dust to settle. Wait for the moon to rise, to lamp the desert in its leaden light. Pry open the hatches (apply more oil to keep the mechanism silent). Raise the binoculars. Catch the first trickle of sand, watch trickle become slide, slide avalanche. Watch the dunes observe their hidden rites (for by day they rest, they labor in the night). Mark where they sigh and roll over, arching their necks, thrusting limb over limb, rumbling, sighing, advancing in their congress, moaning as they stretch awake and yawn, shedding sand as they shake the slumber from their flanks. And when the lightening spreads along the western sky and the dunes fold themselves, lumbering to rest, tired dogs nosing out their place of sleep, set down the binoculars. Fumble for the key, always fumble in one pocket or another. Unlock the leg iron. Apply weight to the counterweights. Lower the loophole hatches (there are two). Fall half stunned on the bunk. But sleep? Sleep by day? Not possible when vigilance, constant vigilance is the rule on the frontier. Rest, but only for a moment, perhaps barely a moment before I . . . before it . . . a falling off of attention perhaps, as if . . .

Sometimes I allow myself to live in darkness. When night falls, I lower the mechanism. At such times, I may elect not to light the lamp. I allow myself to sit, hands idle in my lap. Breathing. In and out, in and out. Merely breathing. Feel the pulse of being. Hear it. The hum. The hum of nerve whining in the skull. The sign of light. Of being and the light of being. I am. I and I only. Here, on this frontier and no other, immured in this redoubt and no other. Fatigue? In the normal sense? Relief perhaps that the great heat of day has ended. That night and the freezing air of night have come at last.

In such rare moments I might call up the parade of years – I call them the whores of desert living – the hollow cheeked daughters of hunger, of dryness. The years of famine. The year the locusts darkened the sky at noon. I let them pass before me, vaunting their lying, thieving ways. I let myself dream of water. Hear it wash against the pilings, hear it lapping, lapping. From where I sit, feel it wash against my feet, sense the woman there, the skiff riding at anchor, the oars shipped in the oarlocks. Sometimes in the half light, I let myself stoop. In the twilight's pale glow, I examine the fissure, sealed now, refastened on itself, a crack now merely, barely discernible in the dirt. Allow myself to remember the year of flood, to see the spreading stain, sweating, swelling, heaving, as if the fissure in the upthrust were a live thing, to watch the floor itself yawn of its own accord. Yawn wide, yes. As if the ground itself had become body. Body, yes, say it, as if the earth were some kind of gaping wound, a ruptured thing, spread wide with its own reek.

Confess it: I have a fear of falling. From the beginning. Terror to feel my knees, my ankles turn to jelly. I never could stand heights. The panic hits me, a kind of tightening in the groin. The thought of it, the thought merely causes me to sweat . . .

Pretense. Pretense and fabrication. . .

All the same, anything not to look. Not to see. Get to my feet, light the lamp, open the logbook, decide between the pencil or the pen. Take up my usual notations. Record my findings: temperature of the air at sunrise, at midmorning, and at noon. Record the drop at sundown: thirty-three degrees in little less than twenty minutes, imagine. Listen for the volley – gunfire perhaps – that signals the final closing of the light. Some distant garrison – who knows? – warding off night raiders, or firing at random. Or rocks exploding from the sudden cold. Mean. Mean reduction of the temperature at nightfall. Plot the standard deviations, day by day, year by year. More comfortable this way.

Sometimes I find myself nodding over the logbook. Sleep? Not sleep exactly. The usual lapse, the momentary failing of attention, momentary at most, the drooping of the lids. I am conscious I am doing it. Or sometimes I imagine cold. I let myself imagine cold, a cold so aching it makes the bones crack, clamps shut the jaws. Or I let myself dream of sleet or snow. Hail, even. Hail in the desert, imagine! The distant peaks capped with white. The melt choking the washes, mud stampeding through the hollows. Then, yes. I let myself remember water. Admit the year of flood when the ground gave way, the subsoil of the fort subsided, how the earth moaned when the ground yawned open. The soil spilled, immense and dark, as if it could swallow, sweep all within it, the sleepsack, the bunk, the field commander's desk, the files. Even the files, all, all swept before it – even I – when the ground, what ground remained, shrank to a shallow ledge, formed an escarpment, perilous almost, and how, chained to the interior wall, I barely allowed myself to see so as not to lose my footing, day in, day out, stranded on a ledge, nearly a year of it, with no thought, no thought of anything but keeping my purchase. Stealing, stealing a look now and again, craning my neck to stare at the watery depths below, their unfathomable blackness. Ah, then, yes. A time to hug the wall, to press the back against it. To permit all else to go to rack and ruin. A year of absence nearly, I shame to think of it. No thought of unfastening the leg iron then. Still now, if I glance, if I so much as glance at the fissure, sealed now, refastened on itself, a crack now, barely discernible, I am drawn to remembering the illimitable depths of the water. When the ground beneath me shook me loose, a tick merely, flapped off a mongrel's back.

Enough. Enough maundering. If I could, I would hobble to my feet, fasten the leg iron, apply my weight against the counterweights, raise the hatch covers. Take my readings: barometric pressure, percentage of nebularization, relative humidity (risible in the desert: it has not rained here in over one hundred years). Or retrieve the logbook from its niche. Position myself at the field commander's desk. Take up stylus or pen, perhaps. Record my findings. Apply scratch of pen to page. Ignore the tick of moth *tick*, beating its clumsy wings against the chimney lamp, hurling itself to light *tick*. Brush at it. Swat it away. Mutter a stale imprecation or two *tick* THWACK. Miss again. Creep on it at rest, watch the lifeless eyes blinking on its wings, two camouflage eyes opening, closing. . . . Then swat! Tip. Tip, tip, teeter . . . . SMASH! The lamp in pieces, pieces, pieces. . . . Now what? Now what?

Stumble. Grope for the mechanism. Apply my weight to the counterweights. Raise the loophole hatches. In the gray light of dawn, hear the first stirring of a bird. The ocotillo sways, but the bird itself is out of sight. Fifteen degrees of light. I call it Day. Dawning now, announcing things to come – one thing followed by another, without variation. And I? In the uncertain light, fumble for the key. Fasten the leg iron. Take up the binoculars. I am grateful. I have my instruments, compass, quadrant, sextant, logbook, charts, a gnomonic projection – of my own devising – showing my distance from the

Capital, my proximity to the frontier. I keep to my routine. Latitude, longitude, all measures to be taken. Measures and counter-measures. Wind velocity, barometric pressure. Temperature, humidity (risible in the desert), measure the mound and loom of sand, the infinitesimal increments that shape themselves in ridge and trough. One moment. One moment yields to the next moment, yielding to the next. One footfall, leads to the next footfall. One step succeeds another. Without dream, without distraction.

Sometimes I think I may have imagined this. I ask myself how is it at all possible, how is it conceivable to sustain an existence here, where there are no roads, no tracks that have not been swept over by the invading dunes. But no: the dunes are there. I watch the sands encroach. I watch them migrate day by day, take daily readings with sextant and chronometer. Night by night, record my findings in the log book. True, there is no telling what transpires to the east of me. And to some degree at least, to the north and south as well. But no matter. I can no longer deceive myself. My calculations no longer allow any doubt: a mountain of sand looms directly to my west. The foot itself maintains its slow advance, soon to sweep the redoubt, all in its wake.

In all this time I never quite imagined it would come to this. Before, before there was always the sense one day followed another in slow procession, day by day, season, by season. A cosy predictability, if you will, without variation – a kind of unfolding, let us say, unmarked by the unforeseen event. My experiments, relative moisture, for example. Gathering sand, weighing it, setting it in the clay oven to dry: so much sand, so many degrees, so many minutes. Weighing it again. Oh, there is humidity, make no mistake. Dew just before dawn. Many creatures thrive on it. The lizard flicks its tongue at the drop of moisture trembling on the desert thorn.

Futility, all futility. Nothing to do for it but give it up. An abandoned project – like so many abandoned projects in the desert. I used to test the soil, imagine! Emulsify the particles in a calibrated beaker. Let it settle. Pour off the excess. Submerge the pipette. Examine the residue. Draw up a certain quantity at a certain depth. The result never varied: degraded soils. And finally I could no longer justify such a futile use of water. Imagine trying to keep a garden, fertilizing, rebuilding the soil after such depletion, cultivating anything, only to see one's carefully tended seed bed invaded grain by grain. In any case, none of this striving and wriggling can defer the slow accretion of the dunes in any way – all that is painfully apparent now.

I used to imagine myself free of the leg irons! Free to roam, walking, walking over the dunes. Yes. Sometimes I imagined it. Skating over the dunes, without effort, feeling the sand, millions of grains probably, sink beneath my weight, buried nearly to the ankle. But a forced evacuation? How will I know the hour has come? How will I set the time, the day, the hour? Now? This night at sundown? Or wait until the moon is full? or very nearly full? Consider what gear to take (there is only so much I can carry – especially traveling on foot): boots, stout boots – to permit trudging over boiling sand hour after hour – compass, topological maps, yes, without question – or only travel by night, so rest by day . . . although what use are maps if the sands persist, one dune after another, shifting over and over, one dune and then another and another after that, ridge and trough, ridge and trough, the sand itself prey to the ribbed patterns of maverick winds, migrating day after day, dust devils whirling in the unrepentant heat of noon, the last whiteness as the eyes fail and the light declares its final triumph.

V.

redound (rĭ-dound´) *intr.v.*, A resounding cry (rare).

Sometimes I find myself wishing I had imagined it – the dunes, the sky, empty without let-up, even the wheeling hawk – a shabby, sentimental prop if ever there was. Had I imagined it, it would not end like this. It would never end like this. The dunes would have lain down, good golden dogs, tired after a long day's hunt, chasing their tails round and round to a happy resting place. Everything would be the same, or almost the same, the daily predictable. The comforts of home, so to speak. Ah, yes.

Gloomy thoughts, and more, many more to come until at last the redoubt vacated, reduced to empty shell, the undefended flesh of its inhabitant exposed, gone, long gone, its hulk a signal to the passerby – if there were to come a passerby – of an obsolete address. Make no mistake: mollusk and gull; hare and fox, whether one wills or no, in the larger scheme all must dance to the same tune. Stalk, pursuit. And dinner. Inside the pit, the diner waiting, poised, ready to strike. The slightest sound, the faintest movement triggers crunch of jaw or snap of mandible. Springs them like a trap. Spider. Scorpion. Tarantula . . .

. . . and you?

I? I, too, perhaps. When the stakes are more than casual ones. Perhaps I, too, in a certain manner of speaking. With this exception: I strive to observe some niceties, stop at dinner – or would have if given half the chance. Or perhaps I deceive myself, after all. Many ways of eating, eating or being eaten . . .

. . . in the smaller scheme? Can you hear it? That rushing, that slow periodic drumming?

That drumming . . .

. . . say in the quiet moments before sleep?

Sometimes. Hear it now and again. Before sleep or on awaking . . .

. . . but that other, that hum . . .

What hum?

Call it a whine.

Timekeepers. Chronometers, very probably.

Those voices?

Voices?

Two voices from time to time . . . that time, cocooned in the nightclothes . . .

No recollection. Must have been asleep. No recollection. Dreaming. Dreaming, perhaps. Distinctly felt it: *plink*. One drop. *Plink*. Falling in the dark. Soaking through the bed-clothes. Feeling for the spot. Wet. Distinctly felt it.

Rain? In the desert?

Listen. The brittle clatter in the darkness, falling on the leaves, escape hatch, on the roof. I asked myself is it rain dreaming? Drumming in the gutters? Distinctly felt it. Touched the place. Distinctly. Opened my eyes to the dark-ness. Touched the place. Island of wet in the dryness. Island of wet in the darkness.

Pretense and fabrication. You heard them. Heard them

distinctly. That time in the sleepsack . . .

Two voices . . . ?

Yes! Gog and Ma Gog, the old story, the Punch and Judy show. Ring open the curtain. The seven-storey tenement, windows all lit up! Hear the sash bang open! Oh, yes, it's them, it's them, all right, hanging out the wash, leaning out the windows screaming,

– Get your kid's booties off my line!

– Your line! I like that!

The two of them, having it out over the areaway for everyone to hear. Haggling, snarling, unsnaring the wash-lines. At it again: the old predictable. Never mind, never mind. You, too. Your time will come. Just wait till your crown hardens. They'll drag you in from the wings at last. Lost. Lost all memory of dreaming, all lost, the desert. The movement of sand. Sighing, soughing like the wind. Waves and waves of it, rising and falling. Crest and trough – like breathing, yes, it was a kind of breathing. Rising and falling, prey to the ribbed patterns of maverick winds. Remember them?

Gog and Ma Gog . . .

. . . your visitors that time, him in his homespun, in hot pursuit, galloping over the dunes. Gaining on her, her bright henna'ed curls. And him running, brandishing his 'staff of office'. And her, stumbling, tripping, falling, hair on fire. SMACK he goes. Down with the net. Now. Now he's got her. Got her in the net at last, kicking, scratching, biting. FIRE, she's screaming, FIRE. But he, he doesn't care. Got her on all fours, he has. Up, up with her skirt, down, down with her knickers. Ogling her rosy cheeks, eyes tattooed on either side,

like the moth that time – remember? – the moth you squashed, all pulsing eyes, giving him the double whammy. He doesn't care. In and out, in and out, the old story. Pumping you up from the world without form. Calling you up from the worm.

Hear that struggle in the corridor? Put your eye to the keyhole. See her in there? Like a egg, she is. All sugar ruffles, pink pastel, fresh from the pastry tube. Smart, ahn't she? Give herself airs, a duchess at the very least, long fingernails lacquered vermilion, pressing the mouthpiece to her gums, pouting-like, pulling on her hookah, sucking on the tube, drawing the air in, making bubbles in the bowl. See her in there? Like a clown, legs spread, peaked cap, hectic spots of rouge, the fluted ruff, the garish wig, tight henna'ed curls. There's time. Watch now. See if you can stand on tiptoe. See? It's them! The hockey team! thundering down the chute! millions of them, piling up in their sweaty best. Throwing their weight against the gate. Bending it, bulging it, bowing it, ***BANG!*** *Splinters flying! The big one there, the fatty, see him streaking through the clutter of shin guards, sticks and pricks, ahead of all the others now, charging for the puck, huff and puff, a hero at the very least! Hurling himself on the shining, shimmering splendor.* ***CRACK!*** *The yolky lake spreading its golden puddle on the floor. See him now? on all fours? lapping it up, licking, licking in there, swallowed up, head first in the mess.*

Ah, yes, ah, yes, the spider bleeds the soft stuff white, while in the corridor the also-rans lie dying. Out there, can you hear it? Hoo yes, hoo yes! It's them. See them clowns, all cyclops eyes, squinting through the keyhole? Peering at you? Grinning? Trying to pick you out in the obscurity? They're pulling on the guy ropes, hauling you in. The winch squealing, the wench squalling, reeling in the washlines. They're sure it's you. You can hear everything they say. See them straining for a look? Row on row of them: painted faces, scruffy ruffs, the smudgy white, smeary red lips, scarlet-stained teeth, red noses pressed to the pane. Grinning, waving, clamoring, pushing. Can you see them now? red pompons bobbing, hurling confetti? shouting ***SURPRISE!!!***

Surprise. Oh, not in the clapping sense. No, more like void, if void could say. If void could be. The sap left bubbling in the swallow's nest. Home to the spit bug. Termite Trebizond.

No light. Not in the root sense. Yet some there. A kind of light. A kind of light-in-darkness. As if rapt. As if being were wrapped, crouched, in an envelope of minute, trembling particles . . .

. . . stars. Or maybe motes of dust?

Not either. Not necessarily. More like lit. Lit, perhaps, from within.

By its own light . . . ?

By its own, or by another. It could be, it could. Trembling, scintillating, hung in some colloidal void. Humming. Some kind of humming. Close. Sometimes close to home. More often home itself, imagine. Nothing like it. All you need. No end. No end to it. In the long run, all you need. Weather without let-up. Climate without cease.

The old predictable.

Oh, not forever. No. Not always. That drumming. Restless, never still. That drumming. That spreading – proliferation, if you will. Minute changes. Hills and valleys, compelled to pull, to push, to struggle apart. Mitosis, branching here, regressing there. Dormant forms, rolling, bumbling, laboring in the night. Certain patterns restating themselves. Over and over. Design of cumulus, stratocumulus, sectioned as the flesh of certain fish. Striations. Minute folds, rise and fall, ridge and trough, ribbed pattern of sand, prey to the whim of maverick winds. Stamp of fingerprint. The pull into being. One embellishment begets another. Lurch into limb: finger and toe, holding fast against the darkness. No lull, no lull, or hardly any. Endless. Hum, drum, darkness-into-light. Can you see it?

Something there . . .

. . . here and not there (because here always). Knotted. Vegetative. Color of heart stuff. No stubs yet. Ridge and bump. Ridge and bump. Over and over. Knock. Rush. Hum. The stumpy lurch toward . . . Presence?

Mine . . . ?

Yours or another's.

Mine then.

No stubs yet. Speck, speck merely. Period. A dot only. Two? Two now. (colon): Speak:

Nothing.

Not in the normal sense. Not in any manner of speaking. No place as such. No one. Not you. Not yet. No name. No name in any case. Regard, then. As if anything were possible. Flight (for example). Wings? None given. And yet, a kind of flight, as if everything were . . . as if no place were here, no where were now. No one was you.

You, then. Imagine: formless. Allowed to dangle, hang-

ing between here and there, any way will do. Fission. Split. Biosis. The old story. Gog and Ma Gog. Welcome to the Puppet Show! Ah, yes. Ring open the curtain! It's them, leaning out the windows, snarling and unsnaring the washlines, having it out, shouting over the areaway where everyone can hear. You know them. You can hear them now.

– Get off my line.What makes you think you have a right to it?

– Your line. I like that. Wait till them hockey players have a go at you.

Never mind. Never mind. Let the winch squeal, let the wench squall. Have they got you, too? all wet? hanging out to dry? Another little hostage swinging from the washlines, back and forth, back and forth, rocking upside down, about to get reeled in. Can you hear it? It's them again, rattling the bedsprings. Always going at it. Never mind, never mind. Your turn will come. The head always hardens. They'll haul you in from the wings at last.

SLAP. *Name?*

SWAT. *Number?*

Kidnapped. Kidnapped inside the puppet show. They'll trim your nails, cut your hair, lull you in a crib with bars. Wear you like a glove. Lost, all lost, the time the world hung upside down, your days of dreaming. Past all remembering. The desert. The movement of sand, waves and waves of it, rising and falling, prey once more to the ribbed patterns of maverick winds. Crest and trough – breathing, a kind of breathing.

My eyes were closed.

Your eyes were closed . . . only for a moment – if only for a moment.

No one could say anything approaching an event actually occurred, something, anything that could be described, not so much a dream but an actual sensation.

Just the sharp drop, the steep and dizzy fall. A well to drown in, but not water. Pure light, with no source visible, no source at all, just the clear light, not of noon. Or night. Or sun or candle. Warm, floating . . .

. . . embracing?

Embraced. As if being could hold, and at the same time swim. Swim inside it. Eyes closed, still you could see. A moment, at best. Waning already. Not to be forever. A moment only. At best. A caul to dream in. But no matter. It warmed you. As if it could touch you. As if it could be touched.

I heard nothing.

You made no sound. But you saw it. A well, a well of light. But there were no walls, no well. There was only light.

VI.

read out (rēd´-out´) *n.*, Decipherment of a print-out.

T**alk to me now**, there is no memory of dreaming. I still watch myself thinking, catch myself spinning webs. But the desert is gone. I have no memory of the dunes, of how they sighed or groaned or turned over in their sleep. Or how, grain by grain, they ground up time into infinitesimal particles. Here, when they talk of it, they say the valley yields the ripest, reddest fruits. So we are blessed.

Mornings here are always golden. I wake before the light. I open my eyes. I whisper my prayer to the darkness before cockcrow breaks the day:

Blessed are thou, Most Holy One,
who showered the cock
with such intelligence
he could distinguish day from night;
who made me neither heathen, slave,
nor woman.

Sometimes, when night falls early – here in the valley – before the door closes – you can hear someone, immured somewhere, in another room – someone, a girl, or a woman perhaps – wailing softly, as if someone were choking back sobs. But there is no room, of course. No wall. No sign of any woman.

Sometimes I imagine – I let myself imagine – it is me in there. I imagine that the sound might be coming from inside my throat.

About the author and this work

Redoubt is Cecile Pineda's sixth published book of fiction. Her other published novels include *The Love Queen of the Amazon*, written with the support of a NEA Fiction Fellowship, and named Notable Book of the Year by the New York Times; *Frieze*, set in Ninth Century India and Java; and *Face*, which was nominated for an American Book Award. *Face* received the Gold Medal from the Commonwealth Club of California, and the Sue Kaufman Prize, awarded by the American Academy and Institute of Arts & Letters. *Fishlight: A Dream of Childhood*, a semi-autobiographical novel, appeared in 2001. Wings Press will re-issue Pineda's novel, *Frieze*, in 2005.

Pineda is an activist and former experimental theater director. She lives and writes in the San Francisco-Bay Area. She finds deserts with their transformative magic to be the most awesome of landscapes. She still dreams of crossing the Sahara.

For more information on Cecile Pineda, visit
her webpage at http://www.home.earthlink.net/~cecilep

About the cover artist

Kathy Vargas is an internationally praised artist/photographer whose numerous exhibitions include one-person shows at Sala Uno in Rome and the Galeria San Martín in Mexico City. A major retrospective of Vargas' photography was mounted in 2000 by the McNay Museum in San Antonio, Texas. Her work was featured in "Hospice: A Photographic Inquiry" for the Corcoran gallery and "Chicano Art: Resistance and Affirmation (CARA)." Photographs by Vargas hang in the Smithsonian American Art Museum, the Museum of Fine Arts in Houston, and the Southwestern Bell Collection. She was the director of the visual arts program at the Guadalupe Cultural Arts Center for many years. She currently is the Chair of the Art and Music Department at the University of the Incarnate Word in San Antonio, Texas, her hometown. Vargas is a long-time admirer of Cecile Pineda's writing.

Colophon

This first edition of *Redoubt*, by Cecile Pineda, has been printed on 70 pound paper containing fifty percent recycled fiber. Titles have been set in Bernhard Modern type; the text was set in a contemporary version of Classic Bodoni. The font was originally designed by 18th century Italian punch-cutter and typographer, Giambattista Bodoni, press director for the Duke of Parma.

This book was designed and produced by Bryce Milligan, publisher, Wings Press.

Wings Press was founded in 1975 by J. Whitebird and Joseph F. Lomax as "an informal association of artists and cultural mythologists dedicated to the preservation of the literature of the nation of Texas." The publisher/editor since 1995, Bryce Milligan is honored to carry on and expand that mission to include the finest in American writing.

Other recent titles from Wings Press

The Angel of Memory by Marjorie Agosín

Way of Whiteness by Wendy Barker

Hook & Bloodline by Chip Dameron

Incognito: Journey of a Secret Jew by María Espinosa

Peace in the Corazón by Victoria García-Zapata

Street of the Seven Angels by John Howard Griffin

Black Like Me by John Howard Griffin

Cande, te estoy llamando by Celeste Guzmán

Winter Poems from Eagle Pond by Donald Hall

Initiations in the Abyss by Jim Harter

Strong Box Heart by Sheila Sánchez Hatch

Patterns of Illusion by James Hoggard

With the Eyes of a Raptor by E. A. Mares

This Side of Skin by Deborah Paredez

Fishlight: A Dream of Childhood by Cecile Pineda

The Love Queen of the Amazon by Cecile Pineda

Bardo99 by Cecile Pineda

Face by Cecile Pineda

Smolt by Nicole Pollentier

Prayer Flag by Sudeep Sen

Distracted Geographies by Sudeep Sen

Garabato Poems by Virgil Suárez

More recent titles from Wings Press

Sonnets to Human Beings by Carmen Tafolla

Sonnets and Salsa by Carmen Tafolla

The Laughter of Doves by Frances Marie Treviño

Finding Peaches in the Desert by Pam Uschuk

One-Legged Dancer by Pam Uschuk

Vida by Alma Luz Villanueva

Anthologies:

Cantos al Sexto Sol: A Collection of Aztlanahuac Writing
edited by Cecilio García-Camarillo, Roberto Rodríguez, and Patrisia Gonzales

Jump-Start PlayWorks
edited by Sterling Houston

Falling from Grace in Texas: A Literary Response to the Demise of Paradise
edited by Rick Bass and Paul Christensen

Our complete catalogue is available at
www.wingspress.com